Lidija Šimkutė

Lidija Šimkutė

Translated into Japanese by Kōichi Yakushigawa

Baltos vaivorykštės
White Rainbows

eilėraščiai / poems

リジア・シュムクーテ／作
V. J-カルマリータ／イラスト
薬師川虹一／訳

詩集　白い虹

UDK 821.172(94)-1
ŠI66

KNYGOS IŠLEIDIMĄ RĖMĖ

AUSTRALIJOS LIETUVIŲ FONDAS

PUBLICATION SUPPORT FROM

THE AUSTRALIAN LITHUANIAN FOUNDATION

Šį leidinį draudžiama atgaminti bet kokia forma ar būdu, viešai skelbti,
taip pat padaryti viešai prieinamą kompiuterių tinklais (internete),
išleisti ir versti, platinti jo originalą ar kopijas: parduoti, nuomoti,
teikti panaudai ar kitaip perduoti nuosavybėn.
Draudžiama šį kūrinį, esantį bibliotekose, mokymo įstaigose,
muziejuose arba archyvuose, mokslinių tyrimų ar asmeninių studijų
tikslais atgaminti, viešai skelbti ar padaryti visiems prieinamą
kompiuterių tinklais tam skirtuose terminaluose tų įstaigų patalpose.

ISBN 978-9986-39-886-8

Iliustracijos / Illustrated by Viačeslavas Jevdokimovas-Karmalita

Published by Lithuanian Writers' Union Publishers

Copyright © Lidija Šimkutė, 2016
© Iliustracijos, Viačeslavas Jevdokimovas-Karmalita, 2016
© Lietuvos rašytojų sąjungos leidykla, 2016

FOREWORD

LIDIJA ŠIMKUTĖ'S work is highly original, separate from any school of Australian poetry and yet convincingly of this time and place. There is a cool appraisal of reality and a certain distance in her poetry, but this is modified by the intimate tone and by a trust in the reader which allows for brevity. Her comments on nature and human nature arise from a clear perception and an intuitively right choice of image and word. The poetry is poised and assured, yet oddly vulnerable too, perhaps because of her reflective openness to the strangeness and beauty of the everyday world.

The unsaid and the unsayable are present within and around the poems, white space on the page equating to silence and the passing of time. Possibilities are opened up by this reticence; the void is perceived as plenitude; and these minimalist, meditative poems do have an affinity with Oriental aesthetics as well as the laconic quality of some Australian speech and verse. There is a broad sweep of mood and tone along with a haiku quality in the spare diction, the deft changes of focus from the tiny to the immense, and the tender yet sophisticated spontaneity:

まえがき

　リジア・シュムクーテの詩はきわめて独創的であり、今までのオーストラリアのどの詩派にも属していないが、極めて現代的なのは確かである。現実を極めて冷静に見つめていると同時にそこにはある種の距離感が漂っているが、それは何故か親しみのある調子と簡潔さを受け入れる読者の心情とによって和らげられている。自然や人々の心情を描く彼女の言葉は彼女の澄みきった感覚と極めて正確なイメージと言葉とを選び出す彼女の直観力とから生まれてくる。その詩は堂々とし、確信に満ちているが、同時に、儚さも持っている。それはおそらく彼女の日常世界に潜む美しさと異界性への開かれた思索力からきているのであろう。

　言葉にはなっていないもの、言葉になし得ないものが彼女の詩の内側や外側に存在しているのであって、彼女の頁の空白の部分は沈黙と過ぎゆく時の流れを表しているといえる。この沈黙にはあらゆる可能性が秘められており、空虚は豊穣をはらみ、そしてこれらのとことんまで無駄をそぎ落とし、しかも深い思索を湛えた詩こそが東洋的美意識と繋がり、同時にオーストラリア的散文や韻文の簡潔性ともつながっているのである。この余白を残した言葉使い、微細な事象から巨大な世界へと焦点が移る巧みさ、自然に生まれ出る優しさとともに難解さを併せ持つ彼女の詩なればこそ俳句的特性のみならず、極めて広い雰囲気と調べとを持ちうるのである。

THE RIVER SHIVERS

under an asphalt shroud

wood smoke strokes
the wrinkled city

A universal quality pervades the outer and inner land-
scapes of these poems which summon up the spaciousness
of Australia but also suggest a northern landscape of the
imagination. So this volume is a bridge between cultures
and a double offering, for bilingual writers offer not only
versions in two languages but also an interpretation and
expression of two different cultures through their influence
on one particular psyche. Whether the English or the
Lithuanian comes to Šimkutė first, the translation is a
recreation which allows the preverbal intuitions of the
poem to find a slightly different form or image as needed.
There is an optimum flexibility and truthfulness in a
translation or parallel version by the writer herself.

This work has a binary quality in other ways too.
There are the various symmetries: feminine /masculine,
light / dark, concrete / abstract, sound / silence. Image
and abstract idea intertwine like a dance. If the feeling is
feminine, yin, the edgy craft could be called masculine
or yang. The words themselves, precise, often elemental,

川は震える

アスファルトの経帷子の下

薪の煙が
しわくちゃの街を撫でてゆく

　この詩の描く外なる風景も内なる風景も普遍的な内容を持っているが故にオーストラリアの広大さのみならず北半球の風景をも想像の世界のなかによびおこしてくれる。したがって、この詩集は様々な文化の間の架け橋であると同時に二つの贈り物を提供してくれる、というのは、バイリンガルの作家は二カ国語の作品を提供してくれるだけでなく、二つの異なる文化が一つの個性に与える影響を通じてそれぞれの文化を読み解きそれぞれの特性を表現してくれるのである。

　シュムクーテの心に最初に訪れるのが英語であれリトアニア語であれ、翻訳は創造し直すことである。そこでは詩になる前の詩的直感が、僅かに違ってはいるが絶対に必要な形やイメージを見出すことが許される。バイリンガル作家が翻訳あるいは並行作品を作る場合、完全な誠実さとともに最適な変成力を持たねばならない。

　この詩集はまた別の意味で両義性を持っている。そこには様々な対称形が見られる、例えば、女性的対男性的、明対暗、具象対抽象、音響対静寂、といった二項対立性である。イメージと抽象的想念とがダンスのように絡み合っている。雰囲気が女性的、「陰」であれば明晰な技巧は男性的、「陽」と言えよう。それぞれの言葉そのものは明確で、しばしば素朴でさ

balance and turn around a core of silence and often take on a shimmer of symbolism:

WINE AND BREAD

on the table

as you pass
shadows cut
　　the loaf

The imagery is sensuous and supple, with metaphors subtly extended as a two-way process: 'at the back of my eyes / the stars in my head / are heaven's keyholes'. So there is a tantalizingly elusive effect. This is heightened by the freedom from dogmatic insistence in Šimkutė's work, as meanings are subtly, wryly questioned – a shape-changing like clouds, but with the exactitude, too, of crystal, and the clarity of mountain air. I think of the so-called four elements: water and air in the distilled thought and feeling, earth in the precision and particularity of the things of the world, and fire in the taut, edgy resilience of the diction, a craft that sacrifices in order to focus.

A particular characteristic of these poems is the sense of space and uplift, while a deeply grounded personal aesthetic and ethic can be felt behind the aphoristic quality of many lines. There is sometimes a sort of counter

えあり、中核となる静寂の周辺でバランスを保ちながら巡っている。そしてしばしば象徴の持つ微光を放つのである。

ワインとパン

はテーブルの上に

傍を通ると
影がパンを
　　　切る

そのイメージは極めて実感的でありしなやかである。しかも両面作戦の様に双方に向かって微妙に延びてゆくメタファーを伴っている：‘私の眼の裏側で／頭の中の星は／天空の鍵穴となる’、このようにここには捉え難いもどかしさが漂っている。これは彼女が作品の中でできる限り独善的な物言いを排しようとすることによって一層高められている。したがって、意味は微妙に捉え難くなり難解となる、雲のように常に形を変えるのだ。だが同時に水晶のような鋭い正確さと山の空気のような明澄さとをあわせもっている。私はいわゆる四大要素と言われるものを想わずにいられない。即ち、蒸留されつくした思想と感情という「水」と「風」、森羅万象の持っている確固とした個性という「地」、そして、言葉の持つ針金のように鋭い弾力性、焦点を定めるためには犠牲をも厭わない技巧という「火」である。

彼女の作品にある際立つ特徴は拡張感と上昇感であるが一方、様々な詩行の持つ警句的性格の背後に彼女自身の個性に深く根ざした審美感と倫理観とが感じられるのである。しかしながら、

movement, however, a questioning of the answer, so that
an inversion circles back on itself to give a patterned
double-take, an almost Escher effect. Paradox and enigma
deepen the mystery as in:

time lingers
on the edge
     of disappearance

where everything
and nothing meet

One word may be used as a pivot, opening a door between two or more meanings as in 'Crosswords / cross the
forehead // I nail a word to a cross', and a deft turn of phrase
can reverse expectation and deliver a surprise, as in these
lines: 'I'm committed to error / uncommitted to time'.

Lidija Šimkutė is clearly deeply committed to poetry,
however: White Rainbows, which can be experienced as
an extended meditation of integrity and vision, invites the
reader to a rich and ultimately joyful experience of the
world: 'Listen / to the laughter of pomegranates'.

JAN OWEN

ときにはそこにある種の反作用、「解」に対する「自問」がうまれてくる。すると逆転効果が自らに巡りまわって、結果、所謂「ずっこけ」あるいは「かさぶた」効果となってしまう。逆説と謎が不可解さを深めてくる。次のような場合を見よう：

　　　　時は
　　　　消滅の縁で
　　　　　　ためらい

　　　　全ての存在と
　　　　不在とがそこで出会う

　　一語が複数の意味の間に立つドアを開くカギとなるかもしれない‘交叉する言葉が／額を交叉する／／私は一語を交叉点に打ち込み’、そして言葉の微妙な回転が予想に反して驚きをもたらすのだ。次の詩行の場合のように：‘時間に溺れず／過失に溺れる’。
　　リジア・シュムクーテは明らかに深く詩に溺れている。しかしながら詩集『白い虹』は正視と幻視についての想いを広げ、この世で最も楽しい経験を読者に与えてくれる。‘ザクロの笑いに／耳を傾けよ’。

　　　　　ヤン・オーウェン

　　　　ヤン・オーウェン：Jan Owen（1940 ～ ）
　　　　オーストラリアの現代詩人。第 1 詩集 *"Boy with Telescope"*（1986）
　　　　以来、約 7 冊の詩集がある。*Poems 1980-2008*

Someone has put cries of birds
on the air like jewels.

ANNE CARSON

The real trick to life is not to be in
the know but to be in the mystery.

STEPHEN HAWKING

誰かが風に載せたのは
宝石のような鳥の声

　　　アン・カールソン

生きていることの本当の不思議は
既知界ではなく不可解の中にいるということ

　　　スティーブン・ホーキング

アン・カールソン：Anne Carson（1950 ～ ）
カナダの詩人・作家・古典教授。ミシガン、プリンストン大学など
で教える。2014 年にグリフィン詩人賞を受ける。21 世紀で最も注
目される詩人のひとり。

スティーブン・ホーキング：Stephen Hawking（1942 ～ ）
イギリスの理論物理学者・量子宇宙論の創始者。

WHITE RAINBOWS

Between one flame picked and the other
given the inexpressible nothing.

GIUSEPPE UNGARETTI

白い虹

取り上げた枠と与えられた
枠の間の表現しえない無

ジュゼッペ・ウンガレッティ

ジュゼッペ・ウンガレッティ：Giuseppe Ungaretti（1888～1970）
イタリアの詩人。ノイシュタット国際詩人賞受賞。

THOUGHTS

wrapped in fig leaves
splash
   across
rhododendrons

hanging purple grapes

wine coloured armchair

想いは

イチジクの葉に
包まれ
　　　　石楠花の
向こうで弾ける

中空に浮かぶ紫の葡萄

肘掛椅子はワインカラー

CHESTNUT TREE

blooms with splendour
     in the courtyard
ponders
on people's lives
through apartment windows

the leaves hum
in Spring wind

shed tears and smiles
on the grey square

栃の木

が中庭で
　　　たわわに花を咲かせ
人間の
命について
アパートの窓越しに
考え込む

葉っぱたちは
春風にハミングし

涙と微笑みを
灰色の広場に散らす

THE DAWN RISES

with its back to the sea

listens to
what the windows
are whispering

朝陽が昇る

海に背を向けて

風のささやきに
耳を
傾ける

A CYLINDER OF LIGHT

falls on the marble floor
blinds flap
coffee boils

Tavener's „Protecting Veil"*
falls on bread, cheese
red wine, hands and roses

wooden shutters
open and close
as late afternoon wind
whines after the sun

*Composition by John Tavener.

光の筒が

大理石の床に落ち
ブラインドがはためき
コーヒーが沸く

タヴナーの「変装用ベール」★が
パンとチーズと赤ワイン
両手とバラの花束の上に落ちる

木製の鎧戸が
開いたり閉じたり
遅い午後の風が
太陽を追って泣いている

★「変装用ベール」は John Tavener 作曲の曲名。
　ジョン・タヴナー（1944～2013）はイギリスの前衛音楽家。
　Sir の称号を持つ。タヴナーの音楽は絶えざる現代世界から
　の逃避、モダニズムの拒絶と言われている。

THE RIVER SHIVERS

under an asphalt shroud

wood smoke strokes
the wrinkled city

川は震える

アスファルトの経帷子の下

薪の煙が
しわくちゃの街を撫でてゆく

SOUND OF HYMNS

from a remote village chapel
spreads through grey birches
                      and mounds
breathing legends

words
like drops of memory
penetrate veins
into a heart space
                      knowing

I will never return

讃美歌の響きが

遠い村の教会から
シラカバ林を通って広がり
　　　　　　土手は
伝説を呟いている

言葉は
記憶の雫のように
血管を貫いて
心の世界に入り込み
　　　　　　私が二度と

戻らぬことを知っている

SKIN CAUGHT FIRE

with pervading music
    the inner engine sparked

burn burn burn

eyes beat into
*Mustt Mustt** rhythm

oblivious to sound

dancers skycraped the floor
through heights of body electric
submitting to the call of thunder
as lightning inflamed limbs

dance dance dance !

*Nusrat Fateh Ali Khan composition.

はびこる音楽が

肌を焦がし
　　内なるエンジンがスパークする

バーン　バーン　バーン

マスト　マスト*のビートに
合わせる目

音は忘却

踊り子たちの裳裾で床は曇り
肉体の高圧電流が
雷鳴を呼び
稲妻が手足を燃え上がらせる

ダンス　ダンス　ダンス！

　　　　*Nusrat Fateh Ali Khan 作曲。

　　　　ヌスラト・ファテー・アリー・ハーン : Nusrat Fateh Ali Khan（1948〜1997）
　　　　パキスタンの音楽家、イスラム神秘主義スーフィズムの儀礼音楽の歌い手。

DROPS OF BLOOD

from the amulet
rest in darkness

the candle burns
regardless

stars
　　wade in mist
the moon
pricks a rose's thorns

血の雫が

護符から落ち
闇の中で憩う

素知らぬ顔で
蝋燭は燃え

星たちは
　　　靄の中を渡り
月は
薔薇の棘を刺す

FROM THE WHITE

of eye

flowers
     the silent
pupil

白　目

から

眸が
　　静かに
咲いている

CLOUDS

streak the sky

sea shore algae converses
with footsteps in sand

waves drum rocks
blinded by sun's stare

boats and seagulls
          speckle the horizon
wind expands the sails

雲が

空に線を引く

浜辺では海藻が
足跡と会話する

波は陽光で盲いた
岩を打つ

ボートやカモメが
　　　　水平線に点を打ち
風は帆を孕ます

WHITE RAINBOWS

in night sky
soften sleep waves
        in dreams

can we decipher
the white page
on waking

a place within a place
in absence of place

I'm committed to error

uncommitted to time

白い虹が

夜空に懸かり
夢の世界で優しく
　　　波を眠らす

僕たちは目覚めて
その白い頁を
読み解けるか

場所の内なる場所
不在の場所

時間に溺れず

過失に溺れる

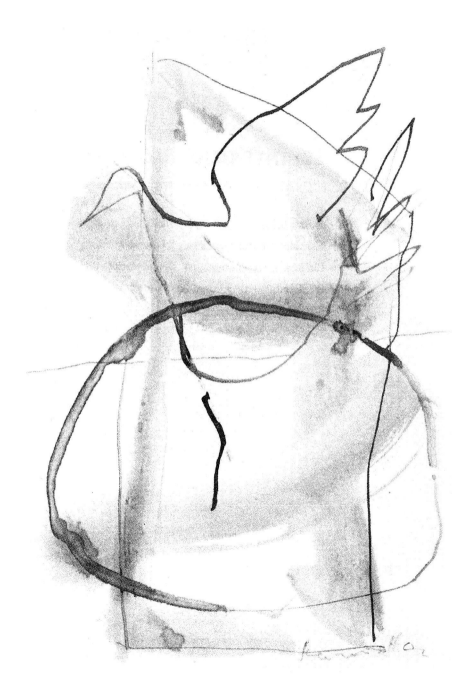

BLOSSOMING SUN

A blue bird flies
From your voice,
Flusters with blind wings
And searches for our tree.

ALFONSAS NYKA-NILIŪNAS

花咲く太陽

青い鳥が飛び立つ
貴方の声から
やみくもに羽を震わせ
私たちの木を探す

アルフォンサス・ニカ・ニリウナス

アルフォンサス・ニカ・ニリウナス：Alfonsas Nyka-Niliūnas（1919 ～）
リトアニアの詩人。1946 年、第 1 詩集『剥奪交響曲集』。二つの根源的
幻想「エルドラド」幻想と、「家庭の心地よい火」幻想からの脱却を目指す。

WORDS STUTTER

a sentence

time lingers
on the edge
   of disappearance

where everything
and nothing meet

言葉がどもりながら

　　　　文章になり

時は
消滅の縁で
　　　ためらい

全ての存在と
不在とがそこで出会う

BIRD WITH BLUE BEAK

picks a hole in the downpour

sun drops its sparks
the shape of lupines

earth's hands
separate flower petals
        while children play
and watch the colours of rain

your name sleeps
        under the rubble

青いくちばしの鳥が

土砂降りの中で穴を掘っている

太陽の投げる陽光は
ルピナスの花穂

大地はその手で
はなびらを摘み
　　　子どもたちは目を見張り
華やかな彩の雨と遊ぶ

貴方の名前は
　　　瓦礫の下で眠る

WE LIVE INSIDE OUR SKIN

swallow thought
dig into the underworld
to open the soul flower

a n d   l i s t e n
to the blossoming roar
        of our hidden sun

I wake to the flow of your breath
in sleep's white rainbows

I feel the way your fingers
touch the smell of summer

私たちは肌の内側で生き

想いを呑みこみ
地下へと掘り込み
魂の花を開かせる

そして*聞き耳*をたて
隠れた太陽の花開く
音を聞く

眠りの白い虹の中で
私は貴方の寝息の流れに目覚める

私は貴方の指が
夏の香りに触れるのを感じる

WHATEVER ELSE

falls by the wayside
             you remain within
the El Greco dream

the smell of certain hours
sift through my pores

no one can force
             me to forget

どんなものが

道端に落ちていようとも
　　　　貴方は何時も
エル・グレコの夢の中にいる

幾ばくかの時の香りが
私の毛穴を潜り抜ける

私に忘却を強いることは
　　　　誰にも出来ないのだ

ONCE

people lived in this
deserted house

sallow newspaper
plastic sheets
wooden boards
cover the windows

tangled ivy
weaves its own story
          and listens

cats wail
dogs whine
drunks swear

嘗て

人々がこの廃屋に
暮らしていた

土気色の新聞紙
ビニールシート
ベニア板が
窓をふさいでいる

絡まったツタが
自分自身の物語を紡ぎ
　　　　　自分で聞いている

猫は泣き
犬が啼き
酔漢が怒鳴る

THE MIST

clings to the lake

trees spread
shadows on water

windows of earth
open shutters to sky

Kancheli's „Exil"*
falls into the pits of sound

*Composition by Giya Kancheli.

靄が

湖に纏わり

木立は水面に
影を広げる

大地の窓は大空に向かって
シャッターを開く

カンチェリの „エクシル"★ が
音の穴に落ち込む

★カンチェリ作曲

ギヤ・カンチェリ：Giya Kancheli（1935 〜）
トビリシに生まれる。ベルギー在住のジョージア人作曲家。「私は礼拝の行われ
ていない教会の沈黙を音楽にしたいと願う」「エクシル」は YouTube で聞ける。

SALT

on my breast

sand
between shells

塩

私の胸に

砂
貝殻の隙間に

WAVE'S SEMEN

on battered
driftwood

波の精液

打ちのめされた
流木の上

DEAD SCROLLS

become
Red Sea

someone reads
the names of the dead

古文書は

紅海
となる

誰かが死者の
名前を読む

BIRDS OF PARADISE*

steeped in crystal
lean to the wall
and point at the ceiling
with seeming indifference

other blossoms stare through
our Leabrook Drive window
        at the creek bed lined
with eucalyptus and olive trees
shading the road in summer

bird quavers scattered in trees
        salute the blooming sun

*Exotic flower with long stems.

パラダイスの鳥は*

水晶の中にはめ込まれ
壁に身を任せ
素知らぬ顔で
天井を指している

他の花たちはリーブルック通りの
我が家の窓越しに
　　　　夏の通りに影を落とす
ユーカリとオリーブの並木の続く
小川の堤を見詰めている

並木に散らばる鳥のトレモロが
　　　　花開く太陽に挨拶する

　　　　*パラダイス = Paradise
　　　　　長い茎のエクゾチックな花の名前（著者注）

MAGNOLIA'S GLANCE

plunges into darkness
lulls memory to sleep
singing of the world waves
over the ocean

I forgot to forget
the rain that swamped you

how can we retain
the sun and silence within

マグノリアの流し眼が

闇夜の中に忍び込み
世界を渡る大海原の
波の子守唄で
　　　　記憶を眠らせる

貴方を水に沈めたあの雨のことを
忘れることを忘れている

どうすれば私たちは心の中に
太陽とその静謐を抱き続けられるのか

THE COLOURS OF RAIN

The miracle is colour from colourlessness.

JALALUDDIN RUMI

雨の色どり

奇蹟は無色から生まれる彩である

ジャラールディン・ルミ

ジャラールディン・ルミ：Jalaluddin Rumi（1207〜1273）
ペルシャ語詩人中最大の神秘主義詩人と言われる。イスラム神学
スーフィズムの重要な人物の一人。

WINE AND BREAD

on the table

as you pass
shadows cut
  the loaf

ワインとパン

はテーブルの上に

傍を通ると
影がパンを
　　　切る

DON'T PULL AWAY

from the red cigarette
          silver tipped
in smoke-dream

this life's fabrication
          drowns
in the stem of a glass

赤い煙草から

身を引くな
　　　　夢の煙の中で
吸い口は銀色

命の織物が
　　　ガラスの
茎の中で溺れる

YOU COME

through the door
unexpected

your gestures
smell of Autumn

your thoughts hidden
in stilted sentences

貴方は現れる

ドアーを通って
思いがけず

貴方のジェスチュアーは
秋の香りがする

貴方は堅苦しい文章で
貴方の想いを隠している

LISTEN TO

the laughter of pomegranates

see the pearl sheen
      through peel

break through the skin
of appearance

let it fly with the wind

open the window
feel the sun and the rain

ザクロの笑いに

耳を傾けよ

ご覧　皮の向こうで
　　　真珠が輝いている

見せかけの皮を
突き破っている

風と一緒に飛ばせてあげよう

窓を開けて
太陽と雨を感じよう

BEFORE I ENTERED

your spartan home
I was greeted by your profile

a halo on the dilapidated wall

jasmine bloomed in the garden
*by The Fountain House**

stairs led to the door
*my shadow falls on your walls***

in the hall-way shabby suitcases

in the bleak kitchen
hung a worn-out towel

*Home of Anna Akhmatova.
** Akhmatova's poem.

貴方の謹厳な家に

足を踏み入れる前
私は貴方の横顔に出会った

崩れかかった壁　映る後光

庭に咲くジャスミン
傍らに „泉の家"*

階段がドアに続く
„私の影が貴方の壁に移る"**

玄関には古ぼけたスーツケースが幾つか

寒々とした台所には
擦り切れたタオルが下がる

     * 「泉の家」The Fountain House はアンナ・アフマートヴァの家
  ** 「私の影が・・・」Anna Akhmatova の詩の一節

   アンナ・アフマートヴァ：Anna Akhmatova（1889～1966）
   20世紀のもっとも重要なロシアの詩人。1960年にはノーベル賞候補に名前が
   挙がった。当時主流であった象徴主義に依らず、厳密な言語の使用を提唱したア
   クメイズムの主導者。2003年『アフマートヴァ詩集』木下晴世訳、群像社がある。

on walls
family photos
your imprisoned son
for whom
you stood in line of repentance

letters
white shawl draped on chair
writing table
books
your svelte *Modigliani* drawing
candlesticks
Venetian glass bottles

poetry's pain and elixir
pervaded
the surroundings

*Deus Conservat Omnia**

**Motto on the gates of The Fountian House.*

壁には
家族写真
服役中の息子
あなたは彼のために
果てしない後悔の中にいる

幾通かの手紙
白い肩かけが椅子に懸かっている
仕事机
数冊の本
すらりとしたモジリアニ風の貴方の絵
蝋燭立が数本
ヴェネチアガラスの瓶が数本

詩の苦痛と悦楽が
辺り一面に
広がっている

主は全てを救いたもう★

★「泉の館」の門に掲げられた言葉

I'LL BE A LEAF

and catch your tears

I'll be rain and
wash them away

私は木の葉になって

あなたの涙を受ける

私は雨になって
その涙を洗い流す

FOR A MOMENT

the waterfall divides

you appear in rock

and on skin
upon skin
upon skin

一瞬

滝は二つに割れ

あなたは岩の中に現れる

そして肌に
肌の上
肌の上

YOU REST

on my eyes
before sleep enters the body

by the bed open book
„Estée Lauder" *white linen* perfume
a string of amber

crescent moon falls on pillow

rain reminds the wind
of parched earth

your memory a thousand and one
nights of bliss and draught

あなたは休む

　　　　私の眼の上に
眠りと肉体とが溶け合う前に

ベッドのそばには開いた本
„エステ・ローダ" は*白いシーツ*の香り
　　　　琥珀の弦

細い三日月が枕に落ちかかる

雨が風に干上がった地球を
思い出させる

あなたの記憶は
喜悦と苦悩の千夜一夜

　　　　白いシーツ：エステ・ローダの香水の名前。リジアさんの好きな香水。

LEMON WEDGE

floats in water glass

your ear turns around sound
to sink a mountain
        in your open mouth
down to a breath-sized sun

tangled vines
climb the wall

fading music
from the open window
covers stacked bricks

green passes through fire

レモンの縁が

グラスの水に浮かぶ

あなたの耳は音の縁を回り
ぼんやり開いた口の中で
　　　　山を一息ほどの太陽に
縮みあがらせる

纏れながら蔦が
壁を這いあがる

開いた窓から
消えかかる調べが
積まれたレンガにかぶさり

緑の影が火影をよぎり

all that my eyes
        have gathered
through the glass
is yours
        and yours

私の眼が
　　ガラス越しに
集めた全ては
あなたの物
　　あなたのものだよ

I TAKE YOU

to my dreams

nurse the pillow
on waking

breath to breath
till no more breath

私は貴方を

夢の中に連れ込み

目覚めれば
枕を抱いている

吐息には吐息を
息絶えるまで

AMBER GRASS

I was a language beyond reason
The invisible air thought

J. M. G. LE CLEZIO

アンバー草

私は理性を超えた言葉
不可視の気となった想い

J. M. G. LE クレジオ

ジャン＝マリ・ギュスターヴ・ル・クレジオ：
Jean-Marie Gustave Le Clezio（1940 ～）
フランスの小説家、1963 年『調書』でデビュー。
2008 年ノーベル文学賞受賞。

CLOUDS PEER

at each other
hum to the tambourine
  of moths

wind prickles rock grass
dressed in algae
fogged sun
   nestles into sleep

there is nothing to lose but life

there is nothing to gain but sky

雲は

互いに見つめ合い
蛾のタンバリンに合わせて
　　　　ハミングする

風が苔をまとった
岩草を刺す
靄に包まれた太陽は
　　　　安らかに眠る

失われるのは命のみ

残るのはただ空のみ

NASTURTIUMS PINE

for snake glide

in late afternoon
boredom

金蓮花が

滑りゆく蛇を憧れる

ぐったりとした
昼下がり

AN ARROW'S QUIVER

over amber grass
            pierces
the water-bird's shriek

flute wind sparkles
over sun dial

the passing clouds
dim and confuse
the fleeting

            of time

琥珀色の叢を

かすめて矢羽根が震え
　　　　　水鳥の
悲鳴を貫く

風のフルートが
日輪を超えて煌めく

流れる雲が
時の流れを
曇らせ

　　　掻き乱す

CLOUD SHAFTS

light the train speed

forests fall
backwards

passengers leap
in fright

幾筋もの雲が

ひた走る列車を照らし

森は
後ろに倒れ

乗客は
恐怖に飛び上がる

MIST

clings to the lake
trees spread
   shadows
      quivering

windows of the earth
     darken
the sound of the mountain
to *lento agitato*

but jacaranda sky
will open its shutters

霧は

湖水に纏わり
森は
　　震えて
　　　　影を拡げる

大地の影は
　　　　　山の響きを
レント・アジタートへと
曇らせるが

ジャカランダ色の空は
その帳を挙げるだろう

レント・アジタート（lento agitato）：ゆっくりと不安な調子
ジャカランダ（jacaranda）：ノウゼンカズラ

BLACK BODIES

of sunflowers
with gold petalled skirts
dance in the wind

playing children
violate their heads
extract and spit out
the seeds into the dust

rip off their skirts
and throw them
on the ground

向日葵の

　　　　黒い身体は
黄金色の花のスカートを着け
風の中で踊る

戯れる子どもたちは
向日葵の頭を揺さぶり
種を引き出し
砂埃の中へ放り出し

花弁のスカートを引きちぎり
　　　　花弁を
地面にまき散らす

ARCTIC FALCON'S FLIGHT

from far away snow

reminds the sun
of the untouched

北極鷹は

遥かな雪の世界から飛来し

改めて太陽の
遠さを思い知らせる

WHERE DOES COLOUR

come from

asks the child
looking into
vacant response

unable to find words
I watch a bird
spread its wings

色はどこから

　　　来るの　と

子どもは尋ね
　　　答えの来ない
空白を覗き込む

答えを見いだせず
私は羽を広げる
鳥を見詰めている

HOW MANY WORLDS

invoke darkness
to witness
the moon

なんと多くの国々が

月を
一目見ようとして
闇夜を呼び出していることか

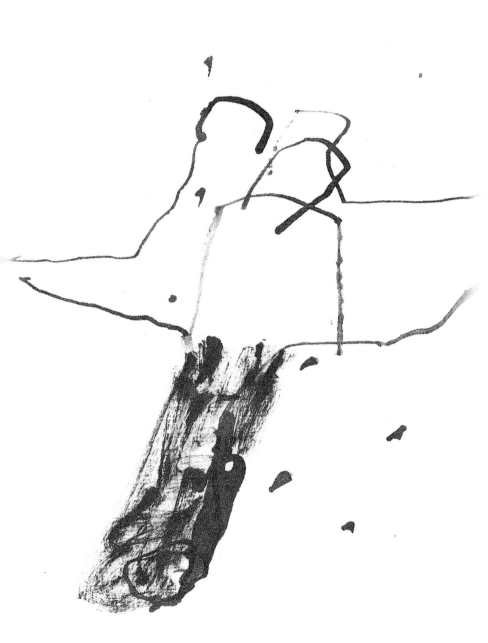

CROSSWORDS

I sell mirrors in the city of the blind.

KABIR

クロスワード

盲者の街で私は鏡を売る

カビール

カビール：KABIR（c. 1440～1518）
15世紀インドの神秘主義詩人。家庭はモスリム教徒だったが、
彼はヒンズー教に惹かれた。

THE NIGHT LAGOON

with solemn palms
        seen in the light
of an alien moon
in jagged sky
holds heavy scent

butterflies dwell
        in thoughts
and pass to dreams

at the back of my eyes
the stars in my head
are heaven's key holes

夜の沼

棕櫚木立は粛々
　　　　邪険に裂かれた
空に覗く
異国の月影の中で
沼は重苦しい香りを帯びている

蝶は想いの中に
　　　　棲み
夢の中へと過ぎゆく

私の眼の裏側で
頭の中の星は
天空の鍵穴となる

THE STORM

strips the blue
     from above

birds dazzle
     through lightning
above the sonorous ocean

the sky's fearsome black
casts jellyfish into sand

嵐

天空から青色を
　　　　はぎ取る

稲妻の中で
　　　　鳥の目は眩み
眼下には轟く海原

空は不気味に暗く
海月を砂に投げ込む

SOMEONE

from somewhere
for some reason
attempts to turn away
from life

or death

誰かが

何処かから
訳ありで
逃げようとする
人生から

　　それとも死から

CROSSWORDS

cross the forehead

I nail a word to a cross
sharpen thought

across newspaper print

across floor tiles

交叉する言葉が

額を交叉する

私は一語を交叉点に打ち込み
想いを鋭くする

新聞の紙面を見渡し

床のタイルを横切りながら

THEY LIVE ON THE LAKE

long wooden poles
uphold bamboo houses

the drifting islands
survive on wispy agriculture

proud tomatoes
        stretch towards heaven
bow their heads with the man
dressed in lotus shimmy
        sailing passed
the hundred year old monastery

pagoda gives solace
to the inhabitants of the lake

彼らは湖水に暮らす

長い木の杭が
竹の小屋を持ち上げる

漂う島は
僅かな作物で生き延びている

誇らかなトマトは
　　　　天に向かって伸び
頭を下げるが
蓮の腰蓑を付けた男は
　　　　百年の僧院を
ただ帆かけて通り過ぎてゆく

パゴダは湖水の住民に
癒しを与える

SEPARATED BY NIGHT

we branch
towards each other

earth opens its mouth
as we plunge
into its depths

夜に隔てられ

私たちは分かれる
それぞれの目当てに向かって

大地はその口を開け
私たちがその深みに
飛び込むのを待つ

THE MONK

in white hooded robe
deep in trance
tolls the bell

the cellar doors open

the hermits walk
        in silence
down the gothic corridors

kneel for common prayer

clasping rosary beads
with heads bent
        they whisper
„because you seek me
I will be found"

僧は

白いフードの付いた僧服をまとい
深い恍惚の中で
鐘を鳴らす

僧房のドアは開き

隠者たちは歩む
　　　　　沈黙の中
ゴシック風の廊下

跪く日常の祈り

数珠玉をまさぐり
頭を垂れ
　　　　彼らは呟く
　„あなたが求めるから
わたしはあらわれる"

　　　　引用文は出典不明。リジアさんによればＴＶで聞いた言葉で
　　　　強く印象に残ったもの、とのこと。

the spider webs
connect their dreams
to whitewashed chapel walls

蜘蛛の糸が
聖堂の白壁に
彼らの夢を繋ぐ

SUN

dissolved mist
    and fused
into luminous sky

roes' eyes met

in tenderness of recognition
melted into the source of light

太陽が

靄を消し
　　　輝く空に
溶かし込む

小鹿の目が

優しく認め合い
光の中へ溶け込む

THE SNOW LEOPARD

scales the peaks
          and listens
to the cry of the mountain

counter currents
and the Ganges depth
echo to aeon

rock flower
turns to the lizard
in confused wonder

          and turns away

雪の豹が

峰々の鱗をはがし
　　　　　山の
雄叫びに耳をそばだてる

逆巻く響きと
ガンジスの深淵が
永劫の響きに応える

岩場の花は
驚き慌てるトカゲに
眼をやり

　　　　そして目をそらす

I SEARCH FOR KEYS

under steaming sky

the ultimate cannot
be put into words

days and nights
shape their reason

私は鍵を探す

沸騰する空の下で

究極は
言葉で表せない

繰り返す日々が
その意味を象_{かたど}る

Man at last knows he is alone in the unfeeling immensity of the universe.

JACQUES MONOD

心を持たない宇宙という広大無辺の中で
人間は最後に孤独を知る

ジャック・モノー

ジャック・モノー：Jacques Monod（1910〜1976）
フランスの生物学者。1965年ノーベル生理学賞受賞。

LIDIJA ŠIMKUTĖ was born in a small village in Samogitia, Lithuania. After WWII spent her early childhood in displaced persons camps in Germany; arrived in Australia 1949. Extended her studies by correspondence in Lithuanian language, folklore and literature (1973-78) through the Lithuanian Institute, Chicago, USA and went to Vilnius University, Lithuania in 1977 &1987. Worked professionally as a dietitian. After retiring divides her time between the two countries and is widely travelled.

Šimkutė writes in Lithuanian and English; published in literary journals and anthologies in Australia, Lithuania and elsewhere incl. *The World Poetry Almanac* (2008, 2010), and *The Turnrow Anthology of Contemporary Australian Poetry 2013* (USA). Her poetry has been translated into sixteen languages. She has translated Australian and other poetry and prose into Lithuanian and Lithuanian poetry into English. Read her work in various countries and at International Poetry Festivals.

リジア・シュムクーテはリトアニアのサモギチアという小さな村に生まれた。第二次世界大戦後彼女は幼少期をドイツの難民キャンプで過ごし、1949 年にオーストラリアに辿りついた。その後シカゴのリトアニア文化センターでリトアニア語、民話、文学、へと研究を拡げ1977，87 年にはリトアニアのヴィルニス大学に在籍し、ダイエット療法士としても活躍した。退職後リトアニアとオーストラリアの二国間で活躍の場を広げ、広く世界を巡って仕事を始めた。

　シュムクーテはリトアニア語と英語とで著作し、オーストラリアやその他いろいろの国で文芸誌やアンソロジーなどを出版している。『世界現代詩年鑑』（2008，2010）『ターンロウ・オーストラリア現代詩選 2013』（USA）などがある。彼女の詩は 16 カ国語に翻訳されている。彼女はまたオーストラリの現代詩や散文作品をリトアニア語に翻訳し、リトアニアの現代詩を英語に翻訳している。また自作の詩をいろいろな国での国際現代詩祭で朗読するなど多方面で活躍を続けている。

　リトアニアやオーストラリアのみならずヨーロッパ諸国はもちろんリトアニアで振り付け師たちは彼女の詩を朗読付きで現代ダンスの公演に使っている。

Lithuanian and Australian choreographers have used her poetry in modern dance performances with readings in Australia (*WWW-Lake George*. Weerewa Festival, 2002) and *Dreaming the Deep* in European countries, as well as in Lithuania (*Spaces of Silence* productions in Vilnius, Kaunas and Klaipeda, 2005).

Lithuanian and Australian composers have used Šimkutė's poetry in their compositions, performed by various ensembles in Lithuania, European countries and Australia. In 2015 Lidija read before Margery Smith's compositions 1) *White Shadows* was premiered at The Sydney Opera House - Utzon recital hall and 2) *Ocean Hum* (extended) at The Flute Tree studio. Among awards *My Father* was shortlisted for *Poem of the Millenium at the Australian Poetry Festival* in 2004. Šimkutė has received literary grants from Australian and Australian Lithuanian Foundation councils.

BOOKS PUBLICATIONS

IN LITHUANIAN: *The Second Longing* (1978), *Anchors of Memory* (1982), *Wind and Roots* (1991).

IN ENGLISH: *The Sun Paints a Sash* (2000).

BILINGUAL: *Tylos erdvės / Spaces of Silence* (1999), *Vejo žvilgesys / Wind Sheen* - (2003), *Mintis ir uola / Thought and Rock* (2008), *Kažkas pasakyta / Something Is Said* (2013).

リトアニアやオーストラリアの作曲家たちも彼女の詩を使い、リトアニア、ヨーロッパ諸国、およびオーストラリアの様々な楽団を使って演奏している。

　2015 年にはマージョリ・スミスの演奏の前で朗読した、1）『白い影』はシドニーオペラハウスでのプレミアム・ショウで、2）『鼻歌う海原』は The Flute Tree 小劇場で行われた。様々な賞の内でも、『私の父』は 2004 年 "ミレニアム記念オーストラリア詩祭" 予選通過した。シュムクーテはオーストラリア政府および、オーストラリア・リトアニア協会から文学助成金を受けている。

既刊書

リトアニア語
　『第二希望』1978,『記憶の錨』1982,『風と根っ子』1991

英語
　『太陽がサッシュを彩る』2000

両国語
　『空虚と沈黙』1999,『煌めく風』2003
　『想いと磐』2008,『何かが語られる』2013

日本語訳（薬師川訳）
　『想いと磐』2014,『何かが語られる』2016
　『白い虹』2018（本書）
その他著書翻訳書多数

TRANSLATIONS: *Weisse Schatten* / *White Shadows* (translation, Christian Loidl, 2000), *Iš toli ir arti* / *Z Bliska i Z Daleka* (translation, Sigitas Birgelis, 2003), 想いと磐 / *Thought and Rock* (translation, Kōichi Yakushigawa, 2014), 何かが語られる / *Something Is Said* (translation, Kōichi Yakushigawa, 2016).

BOOK TRANSLATION INTO LITHUANIAN: David Malouf, *An Imaginary Life* (2002).

OTHER BOOK PUBLICATIONS: *Lietuviški Ex Libris* / *Lithuanian Bookplates* (1980), *Contemporary Lithuanian Bookplates* (1989).

CD PUBLICATIONS, BILINGUAL WITH MUSICIAN, MUSIC OR SOUND INSERTS: *Klausykim vėjo* / *Listen to the wind*, Boris Kovareč ABC radio 2000/08; *Tylos erdvės* / *Spaces of Silence*, Hildegard von Bingen & Eric Satie, 2004; *Vėjo žvilgesys* / *Wind Sheen*, Gediminas Sederevičius, Japanese flute, 2006; *Balti šešeliai* / *White Shadows*, Saulius Šiaučiulis, piano, 2008; *Mintis ir uola* / *Thought and Rock*, Anita Hustas, double bass, 2014.

Eglė, Queen of the Serpents, Lithuanian Folktale, A. Smolskus, reed-pipe, translated and told by Lidija Šimkutė.

More about the author: www.ace.net.au/lidija

Acknowledgments

My appreciation to Jan Owen, Geoff Kemp
and Lithuanian colleagues for their valuable
comments editing the English and Lithuanian poems.

LIDIJA ŠIMKUTĖ

謝　辞

ヤン・オーウェン、ジョフ・ケンプ、およびリトアニアの
仲間たちに、英語・リトアニア語、両国語による編集に際
し寄せられた貴重な助言に対し心から感謝の意を表します。

　　　リジア・シュムクーテ

訳者あとがき

　ヤン・オーウェン氏の序文は誠に当を得たリジア詩の解説である。加えることはほとんどない。

　しかし、何時も思うのだが、彼女の詩を俳句と並べることは如何なものだろう。何もわざわざ東洋の文化である俳句を引き合いに出す必要はないのではないのだろうか。俳句には私たちの住む日本という風土から生み出された独特の風土性があり、それが独特の形式となっているのだろう。ある民族が生み出した形式は、その民族が生きてきた風土から湧き出してきたもので、5・7・5という語数、もしくは韻律、はそれ自体では意味のないものではないだろうか。オーウェン氏がリジアさんの詩の特徴について俳句に言及せず、ただ「東洋的美意識との親近性」、としか言っていないのは正しいと思う。

　リジアさんの世界には確かに東洋的美意識に通じるもの、というか、日本人のそれに通じるもの、と言ったほうが正しいかもしれない、があると言えるだろう。

　日本の伝統的芸術の世界には、「間」と言うものが大きな意味を持っている。芸術の世界だけではなく、日常の世界においても、「間が悪い」「間が抜けている」などといった言葉が使われる。昨今では、「空気」という言葉がよくつかわれるようだが、どこかに「間」と通じるところもあると思える。特に最近では有名になった「忖度」という言葉がある。言葉や文字になって表現されてはいないが、気持ちという空間の意味を推し量ることを言うのだろう。確かに「空間」に全て

を託するという芸当は、西洋には存在しないかもしれない。

　キャンバスの全てを色や形で埋め尽くすという西洋の絵画と、何も描かれていない部分のほうが多い東洋の絵画との違いと言えるだろう。

　そしてリジアさんがいつも見詰めているのは、与えられた枠組みや自分で取り上げた枠組みの中の世界ではなく、それらの枠の間の表現しえない無の世界、空間であることを、この詩集の本体である彼女の詩が始まるまえの扉の頁にウンガレッティの詩行を引用していることからも判る。

　本当に表現したいことを表現しようとして私たちは何時も苦闘している。私たちが使う文字は時に私たちの意に反してその文字自体が持っている様々な意味を表してくるのだ。リジアさんは文字を扱う詩人としてその苦しみを率直に表現している詩人だと私は思う。

　表題詩「白い虹が」を読んでみよう。
「読んでみよう」と言ったが果たしてこの詩は読めるのだろうか。「白い虹」は複数である。この虹は果たして私たちが知っている枠組みの中にある「虹」だろうか。第二連にある「白い頁」とどのように関わるのだろうか。私の枠組みの中に無理やり引き込んで解釈するなら、複数の虹は、広大無辺な夜空を埋め尽くす星の世界と読む、それを受けての「白い頁」ではなかろうか。白い頁を「読み解く」はたんに「読む」ではなく「暗号を解読する」という意味の英語が使われている。暗号とは我々が日常使っている枠組みに当てはまらない記号の連続だろう。まさに「詩」は暗号であり、我々は詩を読むのではなく、暗号を解読しなければならないのだ。なぜなら「白い頁」は「場所の内なる場所／不在の場所」つまり「無」の空間なのだから。

だから最終の二行を解読すれば、多分こうなるのではないだろうか。

　時という正確無比で、したがって非情な枠組みにとらわれることなく、文法という非情な枠組みを無視してあえて過ちを犯すことを選ぼう。とでも解釈しよう。あとは読者自身の暗号解読力に任されねばならない。

　「場所の内なる場所」を「理解」させてくれるもう一つの鍵は、「私たちは肌の内側で生き」という作品ではなかろうか。これは甚だ官能的な世界を描いているが、理性的というか、ロゴス的世界から逃れるにはエロス的世界に入ることが必要かもしれない。だがリジアさんは決してエロス的詩人ではない。言うならば、ミュトス的世界を求める詩人なのかもしれない。

　以前訳した二冊の詩集に比べて、今回の詩集に私は時々戸惑いを感じることがあった。というのは、彼女の詩がときに極めて判りやすいというか、極めて具体的、具象的、描写に傾斜していることがかなり見受けられたことである。そこでは暗号解読の楽しさが失われているかもしれないが、彼女が難解な暗号を組み立てる詩人であると同時に極めて正確に現実の世界を見極める力を持っていることを示してくれて、ふと安心というか、肩の力が抜ける感じがすることもあった。詩集最後の作品「私は鍵を探す」に私は詩人リジアの叫びを聞いたと思った。誠に「繰り返す日々の中に」リジアの暗号を解読する鍵が隠されているのだった。

2017 年 12 月 17 日
薬師川虹一記す

訳者略歴

薬師川虹一（やくしがわ・こういち）

1929 年生まれ。1954 年同志社大学大学院（英文学専攻）文学修士。
現在、同志社大学名誉教授。
「日本詩人クラブ」「関西詩人協会」「京都写真芸術家協会」「NPO
日本写道協会」会員／詩誌「RAVINE」編集・同人

〈受賞歴〉
1997 年 7 月　京都市芸術文化協会賞
2010 年 4 月　瑞宝中綬章
2014 年 10 月　日本翻訳家協会より翻訳特別賞

〈著書〉『イギリス・ロマン派の研究』、『ヒーニーの世界』
〈訳書〉『障害児の治療と教育』
〈共訳〉『フィリップ・ラーキン詩集』、『シェイマス・ヒーニー全詩
　　　　集 1966 ～ 1995 年』、ヒーニー『水準器』、『電燈』、『郊外線
　　　　と環状線』、『さ迷えるスウィニー』、『人間の鎖』
〈詩集〉『疲れた犬のいる風景』
　　　　『詩と写真―石佛と語る』他
〈訳詩集〉リジア・シムクーテ
　　　　　『想いと磐／ THOUGHT AND ROCK』
　　　　　『何かが語られる／ SOMETHING IS SAID』

CONTENTS

FOREWORD   6

WHITE RAINBOWS

THOUGHTS ...   20

CHESTNUT TREE ...   22

THE DAWN RISES ...   24

A CYLINDER OF LIGHT ...   26

THE RIVER SHIVERS ...   28

SOUND OF HYMNS ...   30

SKIN CAUGHT FIRE ...   32

DROPS OF BLOOD ...   34

FROM THE WHITE ...   36

CLOUDS ...   38

WHITE RAINBOWS ...   40

BLOSSOMING SUN

WORDS STUTTER ...   46

BIRD WITH BLUE BEAK ...   48

目 次

まえがき　　7

白い虹

想いは ...　21

栃の木 ...　23

朝陽が昇る ...　25

光の筒が ...　27

川は震える ...　29

讃美歌の響きが ...　31

はびこる音楽が ...　33

血の雫が ...　35

白　目 ...　37

雲が ...　39

白い虹が ...　41

花咲く太陽

言葉がどもりながら ...　47

青いくちばしの鳥が ...　49

WE LIVE INSIDE OUR SKIN ... 50

WHATEVER ELSE ... 52

ONCE ... 54

THE MIST ... 56

SALT ... 58

WAVE'S SEMEN ... 60

DEAD SCROLLS ... 62

BIRDS OF PARADISE ... 64

MAGNOLIA'S GLANCE ... 66

THE COLOURS OF RAIN

WINE AND BREAD ... 72

DON'T PULL AWAY ... 74

YOU COME ... 76

LISTEN TO ... 78

BEFORE I ENTERED ... 80

I'LL BE A LEAF ... 84

FOR A MOMENT ... 86

YOU REST ... 88

LEMON WEDGE ... 90

I TAKE YOU ... 94

私たちは肌の内側で生き ...　51

どんなものが ...　53

嘗て ...　55

靄が ...　57

塩 ...　59

波の精液 ...　61

古文書は ...　63

パラダイスの鳥は ...　65

マグノリアの流し眼が ...　67

雨の色どり

ワインとパン ...　73

赤い煙草から ...　75

貴方は現れる ...　77

ザクロの笑いに ...　79

貴方の謹厳な家に ...　81

私は木の葉になって ...　85

一瞬 ...　87

あなたは休む ...　89

レモンの縁が ...　91

私は貴方を ...　95

AMBER GRASS

CLOUDS PEER ... 100

NASTURTIUMS PINE ... 102

AN ARROW'S QUIVER ... 104

CLOUD SHAFTS ... 106

MIST ... 108

BLACK BODIES ... 110

ARCTIC FALCON'S FLIGHT ... 112

WHERE DOES COLOUR ... 114

HOW MANY WORLDS ... 116

CROSSWORDS

THE NIGHT LAGOON ... 122

THE STORM ... 124

SOMEONE ... 126

CROSSWORDS ... 128

THEY LIVE ON THE LAKE ... 130

SEPARATED BY NIGHT ... 132

THE MONK ... 134

SUN ... 138

THE SNOW LEOPARD ... 140

I SEARCH FOR KEYS ... 142

About the Author   146

Acknowledgments   152

アンバー草

雲は ...　101

金蓮花が ...　103

琥珀色の叢を ...　105

幾筋もの雲が ...　107

霧は ...　109

向日葵の ...　111

北極鷹は ...　113

色はどこから ...　115

なんと多くの国々が ...　117

クロスワード

夜の沼 ...　123

嵐 ...　125

誰かが ...　127

交叉する言葉が ...　129

彼らは湖水に暮らす ...　131

夜に隔てられ ...　133

僧は ...　135

太陽が ...　139

雪の豹が ...　141

私は鍵を探す ...　143

謝　辞　153

訳者あとがき　154

詩集　白い虹

2018 年 4 月 1 日　第 1 刷発行
著　者　リジア・シュムクーテ
翻訳者　薬師川虹一
発行人　左子真由美
発行所　㈱竹林館
〒 530-0044　大阪市北区東天満 2-9-4 千代田ビル東館 7 階 FG
Tel 06-4801-6111　Fax 06-4801-6112
郵便振替 00980-9-44593　URL http://www.chikurinkan.co.jp
印刷・製本　㈱国際印刷出版研究所
〒 551-0002　大阪市大正区三軒家東 3-11-34
© Lidija Šimkutė
© Kōichi Yakushigawa　2018 Printed in Japan
ISBN978-4-86000- 376-0　C0098
定価はカバーに表示しています。落丁・乱丁はお取り替えいたします。

White Rainbows / poems
Lidija Šimkutė
Translation: Kōichi Yakushigawa
First published by CHIKURINKAN Apr. 2018
2-9-4-7FG, Higashitenma, Kita-ku, Osaka, Japan
http://www.chikurinkan.co.jp
Printed by KOKUSAIINSATSU Osaka, Japan
All rights reserved